ACKNOWLEDGEMENTS

Many thanks to K9 Handler *Matt Braden* of the Hilliard, Ohio Police Department, and to K9 Officer *Kane* for patiently posing for the cover photo.

Print ISBN: 978-1-7349030-4-1
E-Book ISBN: 978-1-7349030-4-1

kathrynadrovdlic.com

CHAPTER ONE

Bradley game tonight!" said Gianna. "I know, are you excited?" I said. "*Heck yeah!*" said Gianna as she walked to her seat. Then I grabbed my iPad and went to my seat.

"What level are you on in ST math, Kat?" asked Eli. "Since it's only the third week of school, level two," I said sadly. "Oh," replied Eli. I hate ST math. It's boring but levels can be easy sometimes; that's when it's fun.

Then Mrs. Holtkamp picked up the rain stick and flipped it over. *Shhhhhh.* That was the sound for us to go to morning meeting. I went down to the carpet and sat next to Gianna. "Ok our greeting this morning will be Hickety-Pickety." Hickety-Pickety is one of our greetings that we do every morning. Then we did greetings. "Ok everyone now is our ST block for about twenty minutes until we go to specials, today is . . . gym," said Mrs. Holtkamp.

"Yes!" Gianna and I said at the same time. We grabbed our iPads and headed to the floor. "What level are you on in ST math Gianna?" I said. "I don't know," said Gianna. We both laughed. Our twenty minutes went by fast.

"Alrighty, line up for gym!" said Mrs. Holtkamp. We lined up for specials. I love walking down the halls of the school, looking in the classrooms, seeing all the kids, and watching kids cruising the halls and getting to class. All the people look different; it's so cool.

"Okay everyone go inside and get your pedometers on!" said Mr. D. Yay! I thought. I love pedometers. "Kaitlyn, can you help me put my pedometer on?" I said. "Okay," said Kaitlyn. A couple minutes later Mr. D yelled, "Alright get your pedometers closed and GO!" Then the whole class went rushing at the rack, where the balls, hula-hoops, and jump ropes are. But Gianna and I went to the gaga ball pit.

"Let's play some gaga ball!" I said. Then we both went into the pit with Kate and Anna. I grabbed the ball right away. "*Gaga ball!*" Then I threw the ball down and it landed with a hard thwack. Then we started playing. We were a couple minutes into the game and I wasn't out yet. But then out of nowhere I just fell and if you fall in a game of gaga gall, you're out. Great, I thought. "Kat you're out," said Alex. "Are you sure Alex I mean, I already knew that.," I said sarcastically. Then I gingerly picked myself up and went out of the game.

"Gianna let's go get the jump ropes," I said. "Ok," Gianna said. We went back to the bar but then: "*No*, all the jump ropes are *gone!*" I said.

"Get the big ball!" said Gianna in a screamy high-pitched voice. "Run!" I said. So we got the big blue ball and did what we always did with it. Headers with Hayley, Annie, and Kaitlyn. "Go!" Hayley said. Then she served the ball right to me. Bang, I hit it hard to Gianna. Bang, Gianna hit it right to Annie. Bam! Annie hit it clear across the gym. "Oh my God Annie," I said as I laughed. Annie went and grabbed the ball but when she came back gym class was over.

We lined up and went back to the classroom where Mrs. Holtkamp was waiting. She said, "Now is our math lesson, here are the papers you have to do. One is about subtracting and adding story problems with fractions."

I just wanted to read. I'm a total book worm, and writing worm, but I hate math, and sadly our math block is for one whole *hour*. But I go to the floor for extra help on the paper the whole time. I watched Gianna do the paper with her long brown hair dangling onto the paper then her flipping it back over her shoulder.

"Time for recess. Line up!" said Mrs. Holtkamp. We lined up one by one and step by step. As we walked down the hallway I started to notice more and more things in the school. There were posters about being kind and having positivity and all that stuff. Also the new kids coming from different places all look different and act different. So I looked down at my feet and noticed how I walked. Step. Step. Step. Step. My converse shoes looked kind of old, (because they are). Then I saw the doors open to go outside. I didn't want to leave the beautiful moment but I had no choice. So I ran outside.

"Where's Marissa?" asked Gianna. "I don't know ... *there she is, I see her*!" I yelled as I ran to her. "Hey Marissa," I said as I kept running towards her. "Hey, let's do our handstand contest now. Remember it's not a practice it's the finals," said Marissa. "Okay," I said. We all ran over to our spot to start. "5, 6, 7, 8, GO!" said Marissa. So we went down into our handstands. After just a little bit of time I could feel the blood rushing to my head and it felt like my eyes were bulging out of my face. The worst part is that we always make each other laugh so our muscles relax and we lose. Then Gianna said something that made me drop to the ground laughing and almost break my neck. "I farted!" said Gianna. "BAHHAHA-HAHAH!!!" I laughed as I fell to the ground. Marissa fell, too, and even Gianna laughed out of her handstand.

"Well, you guys wanna practice our handshake?" said Marissa. "K," said Gianna. For our special handshake, Gianna and I run at Marissa, then we jump up and put our arms in front of our chest, like a chest bump but with the side of our arm. "Come on!" yelled Marissa. So Gianna and I started running towards her. "Ahh!" yelled Gianna as we hit Marissa. Then Elaina came over while we were coming down from jumping. "Hey girls!" Elaina said. "Hey," we all said to Elaina. "What are you guys doing?" "Practicing our handshake," said Marissa. "Cool," she said. "Oh hey Kennedy! I need to talk to you about . . ." Her voice faded as she walked off. "Well that was weird," I said.

"Hey guys lets go cheer for the football players," said Gianna. "Okay!" I said as Gianna started running. "Ok players, we're the cheerleaders and I want a fair game no illegal plays," I said. "Uh, okay?" someone said but I didn't see who. "Ok let's do a cheer," said Gianna. "Which one?" asked Marissa. "What about work it?" asked Gianna. "Okay," said Marissa and I at the same time. *"Jinx!"* I said right before Marissa did. Gianna smothered a laugh. "Ok 5, 6, 7, 8," said Gianna. Then we all started. "All the fans up in the stands get on your feet and clap your hands just work it yeah, yeah! Just work it, yeah, yeah!" We did it two more times to finish the cheer. God I hate this, I thought. "Alright next cheer is jaguar jungle 5, 6, 7, 8," said Gianna. "Welcome to the Jaguar jungle welcome to the Jaguar jungle; Jaguar jungle!"

"Ok fifth graders! Time to go in!" said Mrs. Buelow. I was thankful I didn't have to do anymore of that stupid tomfoolery. It's embarrassing and weird. "That's us we have to go in," said Marissa. We lined up and Morgan came to see me. "Hey," she said. "Hey," I said. "Wait one second." "Okay," she said as I walked over to Gianna. "Gianna do you want to sit by us today?" I asked. "Sure, and Marissa will be there too," said Gianna. "Okay," I said.

So then we went inside the doors of the school and I looked into the kindergarten room and then across the hall into the music room. Two ages right across from each other it's awesome. We walked to our lunch cart that Eli brought down, I think. And my lunch box was perfectly in the spot I left it with the little sticker of a dog right on the top. I grabbed it and went in the cafeteria, then sat down next to Elaina at our table.

Our table was the perfect table (at least I think) it was right in the middle of the cafeteria. We could see everyone, and were closer than anyone to the trash cans so, if you ever have an 'accident' (like throwing up) we have the best spot.

"Morgan, are you going to the Bradley game tonight?" I asked. "Well my sister, brothers, and dad are going, but my mom and I aren't," she said with an eye roll. "Oh well, its ok. Maybe I can take you next time," I said. "Yes! Please!" said Morgan. "Ok I will ask my mom later, so calm down," I said. "Ok, ok," she said as she pulled out her barbecue chips that she always has. "Hahaha your barbecue chips," I said. Morgan and I call her barbecue chips 'the usual' because she *always* has them.

"Alright everyone silent lunch is starting now. That means no talking right?" said Mrs. Teske. "Yes," said everyone in a moaning tone. "Hey Gianna, is the game tonight an away game or a home game?" I whispered. "It's a home game," she whispered back. "Girls, whispering is still talking," said Mrs. Teske. "Okay," I said, and took a bite of my muffin.

"Alright all tables compost and head back to your classrooms," said Mrs. Teske. So I got up and went to the composting table: food and paper in compost; Gatorade bottles and juice boxes in recycling; then everything else in landfill, I thought. So I just plopped everything in the landfill, grabbed my lunchbox and lined up with my class. While waiting to go back to class I stared at the sticker on my lunch box. It was a picture of a German shepherd. I just couldn't look away from it for some reason. It had been on my lunch box since second grade and now it seemed like a sign of something but I couldn't tell what. I kept looking at the dog's golden fur shining against the light. Had it always been that shiny?

Next was my favorite time of the school day: literature. I love reading more than writing, but just a little bit. Right now I'm reading "Out of My Mind" by Sharon M. Draper. I'm only a little bit into it, but it's already *so* good. "Go to the carpet for read aloud," said Mrs. Holtkamp. Gosh dang it. At read aloud we're reading "The Vanderbeekers." It's a really good book too.

After we finished read aloud it was writing time. We were doing 'Dear Mrs. H. letters.' So I wrote that I'm pretty good at literature. And not good at math yet (we always say yet with something we're not good at). I told her about my vacation and my summer and all that stuff, just so she can learn a little bit about me. I wish I knew more about Mrs. Holtkamp though, because I know a little bit about her, but not too much because I haven't been in her class for long.

"Once you're finished with your 'Dear Mrs. H letters,' do S.S.R," (super silent reading) said Mrs. Holtkamp. I'm almost done

I thought. I got up and gave Mrs. Holtkamp the paper. "It's almost time to leave for the day. Clean up!" said Mrs. Holtkamp. I looked for trash around the room and I definitely saw some. I tossed a slip of paper and some goldfish crumbs in the trash, then organized Mrs. Holtkamp's marker drawer before I sat back down in my seat. "Thank you Kathryn," said Mrs. Holtkamp. "You're welcome," I said. She smiled at me. Oops I forgot to get my book bag. I got up and got my book bag and my lunch box.

Ringggg! "Bye everyone have a good weekend!" said Mrs. Holtkamp. "Bye Mrs. Holtkamp!" I said as I ran to the door. Then I zoomed out that door through the halls and out onto the car line barely noticing anything because I was going so fast. While I was waiting for mom to pick me up, I pulled out my book. But when you read on the car line the minutes go so fast and in what feels like the blink of an eye your parents are there. So I closed my book and got into mom's car. "Hello gorgeous!" said mom. "Hi," I said in a lazy tone. "How was school today?" she asked as she looked through the rear view mirror at me. "Good," I said avoiding her eyes. We just rode home in silence after the greetings like always. I looked at all the crops, the soy beans, and the corn. It's amazing how all the farmers plant and harvest all of that stuff. I think they have to do it soon, the corn and the soy beans were getting pretty big so that's what I would guess but I don't know anything about farming.

When we arrived at our house we had to go down the huge gravel driveway like we always do. It rocks you around like you've never been rocked before, but I can still manage to see into mom and dad's room and look at my fighting dummies. I got out of the car but I almost fell to the ground because I'd been sitting down for what felt like hours. "Jelly legs. Goin' down!" I said as I fell.

When I got into the house I zoomed upstairs before doing anything. I threw my book bag on mom and dad's bed and grabbed the fighting dummies. I loved fighting. It was one of my favorite things to do when I was at home. I grabbed the biggest dummy, (mostly because I didn't really need the small ones anymore). I put it down in the perfect spot right in front of me, backed up and did the flying ninja kick right into it. I did that ten more times and then I remembered I have to ask mom something. "Mom!" I yelled. "Yeah?" she yelled back. "Am I allowed to walk around tonight?" I yelled. "Yes!" she yelled. "Yay! Thank you!" I said but she didn't answer back.

A couple hours later we were getting ready to go to the game! I was so excited because when we got there we were going to tail gate. So we hopped in the car, and we were off. It wasn't a long car ride because we live like two minutes away from Bradley High School.

"Yay we're here I'm so excited!" I said. "I know me too!" Mom said. "Nice," I said. We hopped out of the car and I ran to the tail gate as mom grabbed the food we were bringing. But nether Gianna nor Marissa were there yet! UGH!

"Mom since Gianna and Marissa are not here yet let me place the food!" I yelled to her. "Ok!" she yelled back. I ran to her, grabbed the cookies and brownies and darted back to the table. I placed them very carefully and tried to put all the foods together and make it look organized.

"Thank you um ... Kaitlyn?" said the person working the tail gate. "It's Kathryn but call me Kat ... I guess," I said awkwardly. "Ok then, Kat" he said. I just looked at the ground and walked away. That was weird. Now he knows my name ... wow that's weird.

"Mom where's Gianna and Marissa?" I complained. "I just got a text from Maria that says they're at Beef'O'Bradys, but I don't know when she will get here." "*What? Ugh!*" I yelled and punched the nearest light pole. "I know, but you will just have to wait for them," she said. "Ugh! This isn't a Mo Willems book!" I yelled as I stormed off towards the walls of the school. I just did handstands

over and over again. It got boring fast, but I had nothing else to do.
I went up. Down. Up. Down. Up.

Ow!! I stood back and turned up my hand and then the pain
got worse. I got a little rock stuck in my hand. "Mom!" I yelled.
"What? What?" she yelled as she ran down the hill to where I was.
"I-I was going into a hand-hand stand and I got a li-li-little rock
stuck in my-my hand!" I said as the pain seeped through my body.
"It's ok honey, now I'm going to pull it out on the count of three
ready? 1, 2, 3." *"Ahh, oww, why!"* I yelled as I struggled to get my
hand out of her reach. "And . . . it's out!" she said. "Wow that hurt
a lot less than I thought it would," I said. "Cool," she said as she
walked back over the hill. Hmmmm? Should I go inside and get a
Band-Aid? Or stay here while my hand hurts? I thought. Ehh nope,
I'm going in.

It was so cool. I was inside the school, but I had no idea where
the nurses office was. Hmmm. Then I saw it. I ran towards it at
lightning speed so, if Gianna and Marissa showed up, I would be
there. Band-Aids? Band-Aids? *Where were the Band-aids?*

Really? There were no band aids at a high school clinic. Wow.
Bandage? Oh ok there they are I guess this will do. I grabbed the
bandage, put it on and voila! Geez I looked like I had a bone out of
place and didn't even go to the hospital because I wrapped it like a
dork. I headed back outside to find mom talking to Gianna's mom!
Gianna and Marissa must be somewhere! I looked and I looked
and there they were, getting their faces painted. "Guys!" I yelled
to them. They couldn't hear me. Ugh. I ran over to them as fast as
I could. "Guys!" I said again. "Oh, hey Kat," said Gianna. Marissa
was still getting her face painted as a little paw for Bradley, white
of course because that was the theme of this game. "Do you wanna
get your face painted Kat?" asked Gianna. "Sure," I said. "Hi can
I get a little paw just like those two?" I asked the teenage girls at
the face painting table. "Ok," said a brown-haired girl with really
bright emerald green eyes, as she grabbed the Q-Tip and dipped it
in the white blob of paint. It was a weird sensation when the paint

hit my face. It felt cold and squishy and gross. I didn't really like it but after it dried, I thought it was pretty nice.

"Let's go do some parkour on the wall!" said Gianna. "No!" I pretty much screamed at her. "Why?" she asked getting annoyed that I was yelling at her. "Because look at this!" I put my arm up so they both could see it. "Oh my God what happened to you!" she asked. "Long story short, a got a little rock stuck in my hand but it's out now," I explained as well as I could. "Oh well ok then let's just go in," suggested Gianna. "Ok, also because I see my mom going in now too, so let's go," I said.

So then we entered the giant stadium. We were under the seats where the concessions and bathrooms are located. "Honey we will be up in the bleachers. Wave at us every now and then so we know you weren't stolen," mom said, and then gave me a wink. "Mom," I complained, "you know how hard I train, I'm going to be fine, and with Gianna and Marissa on my side we're unstoppable against anyone." "I know but just be careful," she said in a tone that made me sound like a little kid. I just rolled my eyes and walked away.

We all walked over to say hi to Hayley, Ella, Kya, Braylee, Amelia, Annie, and Amber. "Hey guys!" said Gianna as we walked past them. "Hi," said all of them to us. But since we pretty much never stop moving at the games, we just went around the corner and kept walking. Then we passed Brayden and following close behind him were Declan and Brendan. When we passed, no one said anything. We walked up into the stands and we passed mom, I waved at her but she didn't see. Wow she told me to do something, I do it, and she doesn't care. Oof for me. After a while we were just hanging out at one of the support beams that hold up the whole stadium.

"So . . . what you guys wanna do now?" asked Gianna. "I don't know, but I say let's just hang here," said Marissa confidently. There was just a pause and then we heard someone say something to us. "Well Hi there little girls," said a man in a white suit approaching us. "Hi?" I said carefully. "Would you girls like some can-" I didn't care what else he had to say. I knew what it was going to be, so the next thing I knew I did a flying ninja kick at him. I did it perfectly! Right into the chest. But then, he looked mad. He walked over to a group of boys and talked to them, and then they came over to me. The biggest one walked right over to me like he was measuring me up to him, but why? I was so small and he was so big; why would he be measuring us up? Probably because he was a teenager. Then he shoved me to the ground!! *Oh my God he is going to get it once I get back up!* I tried to get back up as fast as I could, but AH *he's trying to step on me!* I kept dodging him until ... THWACK! Someone came up behind me and hit that guy.

"We're here to help," said Amelia. "Gosh, thanks," I said. "No problem," she said as I got in formation with them. Then all of the guy's friends came up to us, but I knew we would win this fight. Then the next thing I knew there were noises going everywhere. POOSH! TOSH! STOP! THWACK! POP! BAM! AHH! BOOM! BONG! And they were all down thanks to us.

"Um, miss could you come over here?" said a police officer standing nearby. "M-me?" I said trying to hide my fear. "Yes," he said. I walked over to him like I had no knee caps. "I have to ask you something," he said. "Uh o-ok what is i-it?" I said putting my hands out for getting cuffed. "Would you like to join our squad?" he said putting my hands down. "Whoa. What? Me?" I said, trying to swallow my fear that my friends were listening to the whole conversation. There was a long pause.

"Kat, say something," said Gianna. I didn't want to say anything, but I did. "Um, well I don't really have an answer right now, but may I ask . . . why do you want me?" "Because we can't do all the stuff you just did. We're too old. So we need you," said the officer. "Ok . . . well I'll give you an answer later, I guess." "Ok here's our squads number." "Okay," I said holding the card like it was pure gold. He walked away. I looked around from where I was standing. All the people who were under the bleachers were staring at me, people who I have never seen in my life, and people who kind of look like older versions of people I know. I turned around to see my friends open-mouthed and staring at me.

CHAPTER 2

The officers called me every day that week. Thursday was the day I told myself I was going to give them an answer, but I still had no answer for them. I tried calling them instead of them calling me, but I just couldn't call. I mean what was I supposed to say? I mean I guess I could tell them my answer, but, I guess I just didn't know. What would happen if I joined them? I would have to give up my whole life. No soccer, no singing, no Bradley games. But I really wanted to do it. I would make new police officer friends, and get determined enemies when I arrest someone, wow. But if I don't go my life will be the same thing and will be no different. I had already made a decision that I'm keeping. Now I'm confused again. I confused myself again by not knowing my decision. I smacked the back of my head really hard. You know what, I am just going to call them. Wait what's their number? Oh the card they gave me! Where is it? I see it! I ran to the card and flipped it over, to make sure it was the right card. And when I flipped it over it was the right card.

"Finally something I do is right," I said to myself because I never did anything right, like when I attacked those people last Friday. That was really dumb. But, to be fair I was just protecting my friends and myself. Mostly my friends. Ok, well I better not get lost in my thoughts because I'm going to call them. I grabbed the phone and punched in the number on the little buttons on the screen. I hit enter and heard the sound of the phone vibrating. I was so scared, I put the phone up to my ear. "Hello?" said a voice that sounded very excited and happy. "Yes. It's Kat. Kathryn," I said oddly. "Oh! Do you have an answer for me!?" he said very loudly. And annoyingly. "Yes," I said carefully. "Well what is it?" he said. I felt like he was pushing me to say something. "I-uh-I ..." I hung up. I couldn't do it. What would I say?

The phone rang again. I picked it up. It was Gianna. "Hey! What goes on?" I said. "Oh stop stalling! What did you say to the cops?" Even through the phone I could feel her smile. "I uh didn't tell them my answer." "Why!? You're perfect for that job!" "Don't call it a job please, I ... I ... my life will change forever! What about you and Marissa and Morgan and everyone I know, more importantly what about school?" "Don't worry about me and Marissa! Or anyone else! Yeah I don't know about the school stuff but." "*Exactly!*" I yelled in the phone.

There was a long pause. "Kat, just tell them whatever your answer is. It's not that big of a deal. And, don't feel rushed to do it. You have time." The phone buzzed. "Ugh!"

I slammed the phone onto the counter and ran up to mom and dad's room and punched all the dummies in sight, even the small ones. It hurt my hand a lot, like a lot a lot, but I was too mad to stop now. My hand was burning, and it felt like my bandage was melting through my skin, so I kept punching, but with the other hand. All I saw was blurs, I barely saw what I was hitting. Then bang! Ow!

Broken.

"*Agghh!*" I screamed in pain. I looked over at the dresser and it made me hurt more. I punched the dresser. And put a hole in it. I was stunned. I ran into my parent's bathroom looking for something to help my hand but I didn't see anything. I wished my parents were home. The first aid kit! I shot down the stairs as fast as I could down to the first aid kit. I opened the cupboard and looked all around. There must have been at least a hundred things in there. Pills, Tums, Claritin, Medicine, some red thingy, *where is the . . . wait!* I shoved the scented oils out of the way with my elbows, and there it was. The first aid kit. Maybe I didn't need it. My hand was feeling ... the phone rang. I picked up the phone, annoyed. The cops. Ugh. "What do you want now? I'm a little busy!" I said. "Well I'm wondering, what happened earlier?" He said. "I just ... ugh! I don't know ok! I just can't! I just ... can't." "It's ok if you don't accept, is that your final answer?" "No! I never gave you an answer!" I shouted. "I just need some more time. How about tomorrow at the game?" I said, surprised at the anger in my voice. "Oh, well, I will only be there around the end of the game." "Yes!

That's fine! I'll give you an answer by then!" I said before I hung up.

Well great, I thought. Now I have to make a decision by tomorrow. I'm texting Gianna.
Kat: Gianna. *I have to make a decision by tomorrow!*
It took a couple minutes until the dots showed up.
Gianna: What? Why?
Kat: Because the officer called and we talked for a little and then I asked if I could give him an answer tomorrow at the game and then he said yes and I don't know what to do and I just don't deserve this do I?
Gianna: Wow
Kat: ikr
Gianna: well I think that u should just come up with an answer before then and remember our phone call u don't have to worry about us. We'll be ok.

My hand hurt pretty badly so I went off to bed. I fell asleep very fast.

There's a dog running at me that almost looks like the dog sticker on my lunch box but darker. "Have at him Dax," I said as the dog was running at me. Then the dog shot right past me. I looked over and saw there was a person running away from Dax with a bag of loot, and I realized what was happening when the dog caught the big guy and I ran at him with handcuffs. "Aggghhh! Oh my God! Get him off! Ahhh!" cried the guy on the ground. "Dax heel," Dax got off the man with a bark. "Good boy." Then as fast as lightning, Dax charges at me and lunges right at my face as fast as he can. I woke up with a jolt of pain from my hand.

That dream didn't feel like a dream. I thought. It felt like a message. I heard my phone ding on my dresser. I got up and marched over to the dresser in a slump. I grabbed the yellow case.
Morgan: Tomorrow can I go to the game with u?
Kat: Why are u still up?

Morgan: Why are u still up?
Kat: Well I've been asleep but I woke up from a dream
That wasn't really a dream.
Morgan: Oh. Oof. See u tomorrow ask ur mom pls
Kat: Wait!
Morgan: Yeah?
Kat: I don't think I can take u to the game tomorrow cuz I have
to give the officer my decision tomorrow.
Morgan: What?
Kat: I'll give u all the deets at school. Night.
Morgan: Night

I looked at the clock. 6am. God, I should just stay up till my alarm goes off at seven. But I shouldn't. Shoot, I went to bed at ten last night. I'm going to have a rude awakening in the morning.

I woke up with a crick in my neck. My hands hurt a lot, but were way better than they'd been an hour ago. I gingerly unwrapped the bandage on my rock-hand because it felt fine. It unraveled onto my bed, hitting my foot like a cloud. It looked fine. Phew. I thought. At least I'll look a little normal. I could just imagine every single person in that school. "What happened?" "Are you ok?" "Oh my God! What's wrong?!" *Ahhh! Can they shut up!*

I got out of the car and started walking into the warm school. I felt so tall and old with all the little first graders and kindergarteners under me. I never felt like that. I'm too tiny. Even the fourth graders were bigger than me. I walked down the hall and saw Mrs. Holtkamp all the way down at the end of it, at our classroom. I walked down saying 'Hi' to all of the teachers waiting outside their classrooms for their kids. "Hey Mrs. Fisher!" "Hi Mrs. Scott!" "Hello Mrs. Westfall!" "Hi Mrs. Mescher!" I hugged her because she was my teacher last year. "Hi Mrs. Capretta!" "Hey Mrs. Cercone!" "Good morning Mrs. Holtkamp!" I said as I hugged her. "Good morning, how are you Kat?" she asked. "Good how are you?" "Good. Thanks for asking." "You're welcome," I said. I know she never hears me but I always say it.

"Ha! I got here before you. Take that Griffin!" I said as Griffin came through the door behind me. "Well-uh-eh-whatever," he mumbled. "Heh heh," I said getting out my iPad to play ST. *"Kat!"* shrieked Gianna when she came in the door. *"What!"* I shrieked back right back at her. "Answer. Gimme gimme gimme!" she said. "I don't have an answer answer answer." "But you need an answer!" "But I don't." "But you do!"

I stared right into her eyes, with a look I've been practicing. "Ahhh! Stop! Those eyes stare into me and steal my soul!" she said. She went over to her seat across from me and sat down with a huff. "I won this," I said. "Yeah, you did like always," said Gianna. I said to her, "You want me to teach you the look don't you?" "Yeah I do," she said.

"Ok morning meeting!" said Mrs. Holtkamp. I came over to the carpet remembering that I didn't tell Mrs. Holtkamp about my hand. "Um, the number I pick is ... four!" said Mrs. Holtkamp. "Yay that's me! Uh I want '1 2 3 4'," I said happily, and the whole class starting singing. "1, 2, 3, 4, come on Kat, lets hit the floor, were so glad you're here today! Hurray! Hurray! Hurray!" When they sing the song you go in the middle of the circle and do a dance move. I did some random move that I made up.

When we were done with meeting we had to do a science test and I got a 12\12. Afterwords we went to art. We got there in a heartbeat, and when I came into the room I could smell that wonderful art smell that the room always smelled like. "Oh my gosh! It smells so good!" said Kate. "Yeah!" said Anna walking right next to her. I walked over to the spot where I always sit, next to Emma and Gianna, at the yellow table.

"Ok so today we're going to be painting our clay pieces we made on Tuesday," Mrs. Buscemi said. "But first let's do the jobs. Madison is the distributor." "Ok. Collector?" said Madison. I didn't raise my hand yet, I wanted to get sink and brushes. "I pick Hayley," she said. Hayley ran up to the board and wrote her name.

"Uh ... ok I pick ... oh for sink and brushes, I pick ..." I raised my hand so high it almost hurt. "Uh ok I pick Kat." "Yay! I never get it," I said. I ran up and wrote my name with my only good hand. "K. Noise captain for red table," I said, holding the marker neatly in my hand. Everyone there shot their hand up. "Uhhhhhh ehhhh mmmmm I pick Mi-"

The door burst open before I could finish my sentence.

CHAPTER 3

I spun around as fast as lightning, ready for a fight. It was the cops. The whole class gasped, except for Gianna and me, of course. "We need Kathryn Johnson. Is she in your class?" said the officer. "Um yes. Yes she is. Why do you need her?" said Mrs. Buscemi, worry in her voice. "Police stuff," said the officer. That was a bad choice of words. "Wait Kat you're a police officer?" said Mrs. Buscemi. I flipped back around and looked into her eyes. "Kat you made a decision and didn't tell me!?" said Gianna, with anger in her voice. "No! Now everyone sit back down or you're going to eat knuckles. I have some ... stuff I need to talk about with this officer. I will be right back," I said, anger rising up in my throat and coming down into my words. "Yes. Class just ignore this and get back to work," said Mrs. Buscemi as I walked out.

"What are you doing here!?" I snapped at the officer, ignoring the kids passing by that were staring at me. "You're still on the hook for tonight," he said. "Really!? *That's* what you came all this way to tell me? That I still have to make a life changing decision in the next couple of hours! Wow I totally didn't remember that," I said, still hearing the anger in my voice. "Well, yes, but also, and this is not to make it more hard on you to make a decision, but we got a new police dog yesterday!" he said with a smile. What. Is. Happening. "Oh wow! That's a-amazing, woo-hoo!" I need acting lessons. "I know right! And so, I just wanted you to know that. You know, just in case," he said, still smiling. I huffed out a big breath I'd been holding in and went back inside, hoping that he would leave.

Then he opened the door. Again. "What else do you want from me!? I'm going to give you an answer at the game!" I said as I closed the door. "I just wanted to know if you want to meet the dog," I heard him mumble through the door. My mind got a jolt and before I knew it I was opening the door. "Wait, what did you just say?" "Just if you wanted to meet the dog but, do you?" he said smirking. "Oh! Yes! Yes! What's his name!?" I said almost shouting. "Jax," he said standing tall and putting his hands on his hips. Oh. My. God. Jax!? Dax!? Ughhhhh what's happening here!?

"Wow, who gave him that name," I said. "I gave him that name," said the officer. "I mean I love it!" I said, my voice going up like five octaves. "Thank you. So do you want to meet him?" he asked. "Yes, I sure do!" I said. "Great. Jax!" he said. Then he whistled. Then a savage giant Siberian husky came bolting down the hall right to me. Phew. It looks nothing like Dax. He jumped so high it looked like he almost hit the ceiling, and jumped into Officer Daniel's arms. "Good boy, Jax," he said scratching Jax's head. "So Kat, this is Jax. Jax go get her!" he said. "Wait I don't know ..."

I couldn't finish my sentence since Jax was already running at me like he was a bullet in a gun, and Officer Daniel had pulled the trigger. He shot up right at my face and I thought about my dream. He knocked into me, and I fell to the ground immediately. It would be horrifying if you got attacked by this dog. He had to have licked me fifty times. "Aww he's so sweet! Hi Jax!" I said as he licked me, and I hugged him, then scratched his head. "Oh he definitely likes you. Now, I better go so you can get back to class." "Oh I wish I could say no but, you're right, I should get back. We'll be heading back to the classroom soon," I said sitting on the ground with Jax in my lap.

"Jax heel," said Officer Daniel. Jax got off my lap and they both walked away, leaving me alone, sitting in the hall, doing nothing. The door to the art room burst open and Nate was at the front of the line, with the rest of the class behind him ... and they were all staring at me. "Are you ok?" asked Nate. "Yeah. I'm fine," I said, getting up off the ground.

"Oh my God, just tell us what happened!" yelled Gianna from the end of the line. I walked inside and as I passed her I said, "Nothing." "Oh come on, say something about what happened out there for so long," said Anna, standing in front of me. "Yeah, and why you have so much dog hair on you," said Gianna. My heart sank. I looked down at my clothes and I was covered in black and white fur from Jax. "And why you were sitting in the middle of the hall when I opened the door," said Nate.

"Everyone just be quiet and *forget about it*. Just act like nothing happened," I snapped. "Yeah because that's not going to be hard." "Nate do you want to eat knuckles right now?" "Not right now," he said. I replied, "That's what I thought."

I ran out to recess as fast as I could so we could do our handstand contest. I jumped through the door like Gianna, Marissa, and I were doing our handshake. I spotted Zoey, which means Woods's class is here, but I didn't see Marissa or Morgan. "Where's Marissa?" said Gianna coming up behind me. "I don't know. I don't think Dennis's class is out yet." "Let's scare her," Gianna half whispered as she ran to our spot to scare Marissa. I put my thumbs up to say ok, then started running over. We hid behind the wall of the school and saw the door pushed open. Ben, Brayden, Declan, Mason, Miles, Bokar, Morgan, and Marissa walked out. "Get ready," Gianna whispered to me. "What are you guys doing?" Marissa said as she laughed and turned the corner. "Ah!" I yelled and Gianna shrieked. "Why do you always do that?" I said as I laughed. "You always say 'get ready' and it blows our cover!" I said as we all laughed, and I laughed some more.

"Handstand contest time!" said Marissa. And we all started running. "5, 6, 7, 8." We went into handstands; and the second I did, I felt the blood rushing to my head, and my eyes bulging. I wanted us all to fall so I said something. "Oh my goodness! This time I farted," I said and started laughing, hard. All three of us fell to the ground, in synchronized motion laughing. "Oh my God!" screamed Gianna. "My gosh Gianna it wasn't that funny like ... " *"Oh my God!"* screamed Marissa just like Gianna. "Why do you guys keep screaming?" I asked. Then I looked over and saw what they were seeing, that I wasn't. There was a dog on the loose on the playground. It was a Siberian husky.

Before I could even think about what to do, I was shouting at the dog and yelling Jax's name. I was full of rage at that officer. First he came to my school, and now, he lost his dog at my school. "Jax! Jax!" I yelled at the top of my lungs. His head shot over to see who it was, and then my anger turned into fear, as he ran at me. He jumped up high in the air again as I held my arms out to catch him. I heard my friends in the back screaming at me to get out of the way, but of course, I didn't listen. He landed on me, and I toppled to the ground. I stood up still rubbing him. "Awww I love you too Jax," I said as he licked me and licked me.

"Jax? Kat, what is going on?" shrieked Gianna. "This is the new police dog, that I met when I was in the hall," I said holding Jax. "Oh my God well, the teachers are coming, and they look shocked and really mad," said Gianna.

When they came over I had a full hug on Jax, just to show them that I knew this dog and it knew me. "Kathryn Johnson! Let that dog go right now! *It's so dangerous!*" said Mrs. Braylee. That plan didn't work. "No. Mrs. Braylee, I know this dog. I also know who it belongs to. So, I can go give it back to him, right now," I said, trying to keep my voice strong. "Well, then go do it. I will come with you." Of course she would. We walked around to the front and saw Officer Daniel, running around the parking lot like a crazy person calling Jax's name. Jax stopped walking next to me and sat. He stared right at Officer Daniel, and I think he was waiting for my permission to go get him. "Go ahead Jax. Go get him!" The second I said that, Jax started barking and running at Officer Daniel, and jumped in his arms. "Oh my gosh thank you Kat!" yelled Officer Daniel. "You're welcome!" I yelled back.

"Well, you proved your point but, how do you know that police officer?" Mrs. Braylee asked. "Long story," I replied. "Mm," she said putting her hands in her pockets. "Did you get arrested?" "No! Why do you think I would get *arrested?*" I said defending myself. "Well, you are really tough, and when you're mad you always say to the other kids 'or you're gonna eat knuckles.'" she said with a smile. "I love it. I always said when I was your age 'wanna have a knuckle sandwich?' heh."

"Oh nice. I should get back to my friends." I ran back over to them. Then it was time to go in, so we didn't say much. We walked into lunch and everyone was still staring at me. I sat down and started eating my sandwich.

"Kat?" asked Gianna. "Yes?" I mumbled. "What happened?" she asked. "Nothing ... *nothing happened. Period,*" I shouted. "Ok, sorry for asking. Kat?" said Gianna. There was a long pause. I threw my sandwich onto the table. "What?" I said. "Why are you crushing your cucumber?" she said taking the cucumber-that-needed-a-hospital out of my balled up hand. "I ... I don't know. I was just sitting here zoned out and staring at my, at my dog sticker," I said. "Silent lunch, everyone," said Mrs. Teske. "Ha-Ha," I whispered to Gianna. She gave me a look.

•   •   •

While I was standing on the blue line the only thing I could think about was my answer. I didn't see my mom yet so I was just standing there awkwardly. "Hey, Kat?" asked a person walking up behind me. I spun around and I saw Matteo. "What do you want?" I said ready for Nate and Brendan to come out of nowhere and do something to me. "What happened to you when you were out in the hallway?" asked Matteo coming on the blue line. I sighed. "It's a long story," I said. Matteo said, "We have time." "Everything can be explained at the Bradley game." I looked through the corner of my eye and saw my mom's car. "Ok. I'll be there," he said. "Yeah, ok I gotta go," I said as I ran to my mom's car, and hopped in.

"Ready for the Bradley game tonight honey!" said mom as I closed the car door. I screamed and put my hands on my head. "Stressed about your answer?" she said like she read my mind. "Yeah . . ." I said trying to calm myself. "That's what I thought, but I think you should do it," she said in a soothing tone. *"Oh my God, uhhhhh!"* My mom then said, "Ok I'm sorry for talking sweetie." We didn't talk the rest of the time going home after that. I was thinking about Jax even though we were having a conversation. So I smacked myself. "Ouch," I whispered under my breath.

Get out of your stupid head Kat. I thought. You need to work on your moves right now. You're a little dusty.

I was doing a bunch of flying ninja kicks, when my mom walked in the room. "You ok, Kat?" she said. "I'm fine. Why do people keep asking me that?" I shouted as my hand hurt, while I was punching my dummies. Mom then said, "Ok you know what, I'm making matters worse, so I'm just going to go back downstairs." When she said that I thought it sounded pretty good. She was walking out, then she said, "And you have to get ready for the game." When she said that it made my hand hurt, a *lot*. I think when I got mad it made it hurt. I ran over to my room because she was right, I did need to get ready. "Wait, mom! What theme is this game?!" I shouted at the top of the stairs. "Its tropical theme!" she yelled over in the living room. "Ok!"

I started planning out what I should do. I also ran downstairs and grabbed a bandage for my broken-dresser hand, and drew some birds and pineapples on it. I grabbed an old jumper that I got from our trip to Hawaii last year. I snatched up some bracelets that had Hawaiian flowers on them, and I was set. "Mom, let's go!" I said as I ran down the stairs. "Ok, get in the car!" she said starting up the engine. "I'm in. I'm in," I said. I was watching out the window, and watching everything zooming by. I squished my face up against the window and I saw Bradley High School. I remembered that tonight I have to not fall asleep, because I could have another dream/vision about Dax or Jax. Or any other dog I happen to meet tonight. Because you know, you'll never know what will happen at a game when you walk around the second time. Or first time. Or any time, I guess. I always used to just sit in the bleachers and wave at my friends. And now that I got an opportunity to walk around, this happened. My whole entire awesome life got flipped upside down and spun around and dizzy from my own stupid thoughts.

"Ok, Kat come on lets go tail gate!" said mom snapping me out of my thoughts. "I'm coming," I said slowly getting out of the car. I knew she knew that I was thinking really hard and she was trying to snap me out of it. But it wasn't working. I just, I knew what my answer was and I was sticking with it, but it's the thing that was fogging my mind when I tried to think about something else.

"Hey, Kat!" to my surprise Gianna was standing I front of me. "Oh, wow, Hi," I said tiredly. "So ... what's your ans ... " "Gianna if you say 'answer' I swear to God that I'm going to smack you right now," I snapped. She didn't make a sound. I guess I was so stressed about my answer that I wanted to get it off my mind and not talk about it. "Well, Kat I love your jumper, where did you get it?" said Marissa awkwardly. "Hawaii," I said. She looked surprised. "Ok well then I definitely can't get it," she said letting out a sigh.

Then we were just standing there. It felt weird. I didn't know what to say, and I bet they didn't know what to say ether. So all I did was run over to the food table, grabbed a piece of pizza, and then came back over. It felt like there was just an odd hum around us. Like the world faded out and it was just us, avoiding each other's eyes.

"Let's just go inside," said Gianna out of nowhere. "Yeah we should do that," said Marissa, giving Gianna a look that said, 'thank you.' We all started walking under the bleachers and I saw mom shoot right past me, going to our seats, I assume. I guess she really trusts me from what happened last Friday. I would too, if I were her. Or anyone who saw me fighting all those guys that day. That's probably one of the reasons the cops wanted me. Because you can trust me. People say that all the time about me, like one time I remember I overheard someone telling a new kid at our school: If Kat says, "Trust Me," you know her word is good. Which is odd, because when I look in the mirror I don't see a trustworthy person. I see a blonde-haired girl, with rich green and blue eyes, whose life was perfect, until the cops entered my life.

"Hey guys, you hungry? I got some money for concessions," said Gianna pulling out some money from her miniature backpack. "Uh, yeah I could eat," I said as my mind was still racing every single thought I had, and no one has won yet. "No I think I'm good," said Marissa as we hopped in line. *I can't even believe what has be ...* "Ok, Kat what do you want?" Gianna said so I couldn't start another thinking train again and stay in the moment. "Um I want a soft pretzel, I guess," I said. "Ok we would like one water, one cotton candy, and one soft pretzel," said Gianna to the lady working the booth. "Do you want cheese on the pretzel?" said the lady blowing up a bubble with her gum. "Oh God no, I hate cheese on soft pretzels," I said. "Oh, we got a brassy one here," said the lady giving me a look. "Yeah, I got a lot of brass," I said giving her the look right back. "You better hope I don't poison your food for that," she said. "I wouldn't care if you did, because I would sue you for it," I snapped. "Alright, here's your pretzel, your water, and your cotton candy," said a guy that popped out of nowhere. "It's ten bucks," said the lady. "Perfect, that's all the money I have," said Gianna. She put the money down on the table, and the lady swiftly grabbed it.

We walked away and my mind was still racing with my thoughts, but there was a new racer. The concessions lady was in first. And she was definitely playing to win. We started walking up the metal steps to where the bleachers were. "Hey guys, are we actually gonna watch the game?" I asked them, trying to find my brother on the field. "Pfft. No," said Gianna looking at me like I was crazy. "Yeah why would we do that?" said Marissa obviously taking Gianna's side. God they are really messed up. We're at a football game then, for what? To walk around and act like cute sweet girls? Gross. I'd rather slam my tongue in a car door than act like a cute sweet little princess. "Uh 'cause we are kind of at a football game. What else are we gonna do than watch the actual game?" I said standing by my previous question. "And also, our brothers are out there. Shouldn't we watch them?" I said as Gianna looked for her brother. "Well, ok! Let's do a cheer for them!" said Gianna. *No, no, no, oh God noooo! Say no to them, I know you hate it.* "Why do we have to do a cheer for them? I mean can we just yell their names when they're called on the loudspeaker?" I pleaded. But they had already started.

"Welcome to the jaguar jungle! Welcome to the jaguar jungle! Jaguar! Jungle!" they both chanted doing the dance to go with it. So I put my back up against the fence, and slid down in embarrassment and despair. I closed my eyes as they started the next cheer.

Five long minutes later they stopped cheering. I wanted to make sure that they were really done, so I still sat there with my eyes closed for a few seconds. Then I popped them open. Yes, Gianna and Marissa were done, but, the thing that was catching my eye, almost right in front of me, coming up the metal stairs was the cops.

CHAPTER 4

I screamed. He was right there, coming up the stairs with Jax next to him. I couldn't even believe it with my own eyes he was right there, *right there!* I got up as fast as I could, from sitting there for what felt like years. I ran as fast as I could over to the student section. But I was too late. Officer Daniel already saw me when I got up.

"Hey Kat, wait!" he yelled, as I trudged towards the students section. "Hey, Jax go get her!" he said. *Oh my God!* Is he *really* sending Jax after me!? I turned around and it was true, Jax was running at me. I saw the surprised look on my friends' faces as they started running after Jax, (so he doesn't attack me) and they were also running after me, (so they can get me to tell Officer Daniel my answer). I looked over at Officer Daniel and it was like a bowling ball hit my stomach. He was running after my friends, (to get them to stop running after Jax).

In that moment in time, I realized one thing ... that this was a wild Kat chase. And I was winning, (for now). I continued running to the student section, and I jumped in. I plowed through kids who had the most terrified expression on their faces, seeing what was happening. Some of them even recognized me from last Friday. Those ones were easy to spot, because most of them were going, "It's her!!" "She's the girl I told you about from last Friday!" and most of them were just screaming about how big Jax was, and apparently how small I was.

I finally got out of the student section. I looked behind me and I didn't see Jax. Those kids must have started to pet him. I knew he loves attention and licking. Man, he probably loved it in there. Well, one down, three to go. I started thinking of ways to get Gianna distracted, because I knew she would be the easiest. I turned the corner looking back at the student section, I saw Gianna and Marissa coming out of it, then, following close behind, was Officer Daniel. He was easy to spot, because all the students were shying out of his way. But I still didn't see Jax. I was 100% sure that Officer Daniel would have grabbed him. Where did he go? Did I really want to know the answer to that? Then, the worst thought hit me like a locomotive. What if he ran on the football field?!

I ran up to the metal fence. I saw something moving like a cloud of black and white shiny fur. "Jax!!! Jax!!" I screamed at the top of my lungs. But he was already making his way onto the football field. I peered behind me and I saw Gianna, Marissa, and Officer Daniel spot me, and start up their engines for the final lap. So there was one thing left to do. Win the race.

I hopped over the metal fence and started running. I didn't know where yet but I was about to find out. I started running towards the football field while Jax was just jumping on it. "Jax, come here right now!" I yelled vigorously. I clapped my hands, I made weird noises, but the truth was, I had to jump on that field and grab Jax myself. So that's what I was going to do. I kept running pretty much as fast as I could, onto the football field. I dodged players, and I kept looking for the white and black bullet. Then I saw him. He was running after the player with the ball at top speed. So I turned on full speed and let it rip. I ran straight at the player, *"Dude, listen to me! You need to stop running!"* I yelled at him. "Why?" he said dryly. It occurred to me that he might not have even seen Jax. "Just look behind you!" I said. He looked, and immediately stopped running. That made Jax stop running, too. I trotted over to Jax and grabbed his collar. "Come on Jax," I said trudging him along. He barked in exchange. His collar managed to slip out of my grip, but he was already too interested in me to care about the players.

"Hey look at the dog tamer over here, and a great football player, dodger," said Gianna as I walked up to them and gave Jax back to Officer Daniel. "Yeah, and man that was fun. I loved it. And I want more of it," I said proudly. Officer Daniel chimed in. "Well, I know you've been stressed about one thing since last Friday. Are you ready to let that stress right off your shoulder?" "Ok fine, I'll tell you what my answer is," I said building up suspense. "After this long, one-week long race. I hurt my hand; I hurt my other hand too. I had creepy visions and dreams about being a cop. And the whole time I had the answer locked in my brain. I don't know why, but I stressed over this so much when the whole time I was winning the race," I said inhaling. "Yes," I said. "Wait, Kat really!? You're gonna do it? You're gonna become a police officer?" said Officer Daniel. "Yes, did I not just say that?" I said hugging Officer Daniel, then Gianna. "Kat!! Oh my God! I knew you would make the right choice! I'm just glad it was yes!" said Gianna. "Kat, I'm so happy for you! But can I come to work with you sometime?" said Marissa. "Of course! Gosh, I would make you even if you didn't ask," I said. "Well Officer Daniel, when do I start?" I said happily. "You start tomorrow at 7 am sharp. I know it's early but you'll get used to it," said Officer Daniel shrugging. "Ok."

•   •   •

I woke up at 6am, and did all the stuff I needed to do. I hopped in the car and mom turned on the radio. "Last night at the Hilliard Bradley Jaguars football game, a giant Siberian Husky jumped onto the field and started chasing the running back. A heroic girl ran out onto the field and grabbed the dog. Later, we heard the police tell us this girl goes by the name Kathryn Johnson, and she is also a police officer. That dog was one of their K9 dogs on the loose," said the person on the radio. "Isn't that so cool, sweetie! They're talking about you!" said mom turning up the volume. "Reporters say that she came out of nowhere, just jumping onto the field and telling Andrew West, the running back, to stop running and look behind him. He looked, Kathryn grabbed the dog, and ran off the field," said the person with a rich, clear, voice.

"Man, why do they have to use my real name? I like the name people started calling me when I was in first grade," I said looking in the distance, and I saw the police station. "Or you could get used to the name I gave you when you were born," said mom pulling into the parking lot. "Well ... mehh," I said getting out of the car. "Well, bye!" I said. "Bye! Have a great time!" she said.

I shut the door and walked over to where a lot of police officers were standing. "Hey Officer Daniel!" I yelled over to him. Jax was somehow sitting on his lap. "Oh hello, Kat! I'm so glad to see you here. Go ahead, take a chair," he said as I sat down in a chair. "So, Bryan and Randy, this is our new recruit, Kat," said Officer Daniel. "Oh it's the girl you been talkin' about for weeks. Hey Kat. Glad you're here, I'm Randy," said Officer Randy. "Nice to meet you," I said. "Howdy, Kat. I'm Bryan. I hope you enjoy being a cop," said Officer Bryan. "I hope I will. Nice to meet you," I said kind of awkwardly.

"Well, Kat, would you like to meet your very own K9 Police Dog?" said Officer Daniel. I was very surprised when he said that. "I get my own dog!?" I said happily. "Well of course you do, all police officers that seem ready get a dog, get one. And you saved this big boy yesterday," said Officer Daniel shaking Jax's fur. "So, would like to meet him?" he asked. "Of course of course. But, what's his name?" I asked, but I knew what I was going to hear. "His name is, Dax," said Officer Daniel hugging Jax. "Wait, are you serious!? That's really his name?!" I said confused. "Yep. Dax, come here boy!" yelled Officer Daniel.

Right then, a giant beautiful German shepherd came through the door. A German shepherd that looked *exactly* like the dog sticker on my lunch box.

ABOUT THE AUTHOR

Kat Drovdlic lives in Hilliard, OH with her mom, dad, two brothers, dog Buffy, and ducks Elwood and Lola. Kat enjoys reading, horseback riding, and singing.

As of 2021 Kat is in the eighth grade, and wrote **Kat and the K9** in the sixth grade while attending Darby Creek Elementary School.

Her love of dogs and Football Friday Nights were the inspiration for this book.

www.ingramcontent.com/pod-product-compliance
Lightning Source LLC
Chambersburg PA
CBHW011153190726
48288CB00010B/3298